AR 4.4

D0484131

FRED BOWEN series
SPORTS STORY

OUT OF BOUNDS

FRED BOWEN

PEACHTREE
ATLANTA

Published by
PEACHTREE PUBLISHERS
1700 Chattahoochee Avenue
Atlanta, Georgia 30318-2112
www.peachtree-online.com

Cover design by Tom Gonzalez and Nicola Carmack
Composition by Melanie McMahon Ives

Printed in June 2015 by RR Donnelley and Sons in Harrisonburg, VA, U. S. A.
10 9 8 7 6 5 4 3 2 1
First Edition

Library of Congress Cataloging-in-Publication Data

Bowen, Fred.
  Out of bounds / Fred Bowen.
      pages cm
  Summary: Eighth-grade soccer forward Nate Osborne and his teammates are highly competitive but, with help from his soccer-playing aunt, Nate begins to see that good sportsmanship is more important than winning. Includes a recipe for oatmeal chocolate chip cookies and the real story behind the novel.
  ISBN 978-1-56145-845-5 (hardcover)
  ISBN 978-1-56145-894-3 (trade paperback)
  [1. Soccer—Fiction. 2. Competition (Psychology)—Fiction. 3. Sportsmanship—Fiction.] I. Title.
  PZ7.B6724Out 2015
  [Fic]—dc23
                                2015002406

For Peggy, again and always

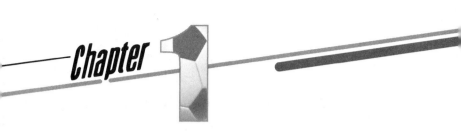

Racing down the sideline, Nate Osborne glanced over his shoulder at the soccer ball soaring through the crisp, clear September air. The ball bounced once at his side. With a quick touch, Nate brought it under control with his right foot.

A defender stepped up to challenge him. Nate had to make a quick decision. He could either dribble the ball deeper into the corner or cut toward the center of the field and the goal.

Be aggressive, he thought. *Take it to the middle.*

Nate crossed the ball to his left foot and cut sharply to the goal. His quick feet put the defender off balance and a step behind.

Another defender raced over to cut off Nate's path to the goal.

Nate slipped the ball past the charging defender and stepped over his flying tackle. Out of the corner of his eye, he spied the goalkeeper coming out to cut down the angle. With a quick stutter step, Nate caught up with the ball and set up a right-footed shot.

Boom! The ball curved around the diving keeper and rocketed toward the near post.

Thunk! The ball hit the silver metal post and skittered across the front of the goal. A defender blasted the ball away from the net and over the sideline.

Tweeeeeet!

Coach Lyn's whistle brought the action to a halt. "Great play, Nate!" he shouted. "That's how we stay aggressive! Attack the goal. That's what we want our forwards to do." The coach turned to the defenders. "Remember, don't challenge someone with Nate's speed too much. Play the angles. You can't let him get behind you."

Coach Lyn waved his arms toward the

sidelines. "That's enough for today. Good practice. Let's get some water."

The Strikers gathered around a big orange plastic bucket and dipped paper cups into the ice-cold water.

"Hey, at least take your gloves off!" yelled Sergio Hernandez, the Strikers midfielder and Nate's best friend. He was pointing at Cameron Wallace, the team's goalkeeper. "They're filthy."

Nate gulped the water so fast that some ran down his chin and splashed onto his shirt. The cold water felt good. The September heat had turned Nate's uniform into a sweaty second skin. Summer was still hanging on.

"Man, Nate totally faked Cam out with that awesome move," Sergio said, still teasing the goalkeeper.

Cam grinned. "You're so wrong. I had it all the way."

Sergio wasn't having any of that. "Oh, so you knew the ball was going to hit the post?"

"Absolutely," Cam insisted. "Don't you

know the goalposts are a keeper's best friends?"

Sergio laughed. "And I guess you *wanted* the ball to be bouncing around in front of the net?"

Stevie Greenwald, the Strikers' top defender, stepped forward. "No worries, I had Cam's back."

Nate decided to get in on the fun. "By the way, Sergio. Where were you on that play? I thought a midfielder like you would be right on the spot to pick up an easy goal."

"Yeah," Stevie agreed. "You should have been on that ball."

Sergio paused. He didn't have a quick answer for that one. "Maybe I didn't want to run up the score and embarrass my teammates," he said finally.

All the Strikers laughed.

"Seriously," Sergio said. "I was trying to be a good sport."

"Yeah, right," Nate said, still chuckling. Sergio was a terrific midfielder and probably the most competitive player on a team full of competitors.

"Listen up, Strikers!" Coach Lyn strode toward the circle of players with a stack of papers in his hand. "Good practice. We've got one more before our first game."

"Are those the schedules?" Sergio asked.

Coach nodded and started handing out sheets of paper. "Yeah. All the games are on Saturdays at the SoccerPlex. Make sure you get there twenty minutes early to warm up. At *least* twenty minutes early."

Nate grabbed a schedule and looked down the list of teams and games. He was looking for only one thing.

Date	Opponent	Time
September 12	Sharks	Noon
September 19	Vipers	1:30 p.m.
September 26	United	3:00 p.m.
October 3	Devils	9:00 a.m.
October 10	Sabres	10:30 a.m.
October 17	Rapids	3:00 p.m.
October 24	Monarchs	1:30 p.m.
October 31	Rush	10:30 a.m.
November 7	Barracudas	Noon
November 14	Championship game	TBA

All games will be played at the SoccerPlex.

The first- and second-place team in the standings after the regular season will play in the championship game.

Sergio looked over Nate's shoulder. "When do we play the Monarchs?" he asked, reading Nate's mind.

"October twenty-fourth," Nate said, his eyes resting on a single line in the schedule. "The seventh week of the season."

Sergio was studying his own schedule sheet now. "It's good we play them later in the season," he said. "It'll probably be for the championship...again."

"The two top teams from the regular season play a separate game for the championship," Nate said, pointing at the last line of the schedule. "You know that."

"But anytime the Strikers play the Monarchs it's a big game," Sergio said. "A championship game."

"Right," Nate agreed.

The two friends started walking home. They lived on the same street not far from the soccer practice field. As always, they talked about soccer and the Strikers.

"I'm still mad we lost to the Monarchs in overtime last year," Sergio said. "That cost us the U-13 league championship."

"But we were the U-12 champs," Nate reminded him.

"So I guess we're tied."

"And this year we'll break the tie."

"Yeah." Sergio smiled. "I'm already looking forward to the twenty-fourth."

The boys turned on to their street. "Don't forget the other games," Nate cautioned his friend. "The Devils and the Sabres are good too. So's the United."

"No worries."

Nate paused. "We may need you to score more goals if we're gonna beat those guys," he said. "Like the easy one in front of the net today."

"I'm telling you—"

Nate cut his friend off. "Oh yeah, I forgot. You were trying to be a good sport."

Even Sergio had to laugh this time.

"See you tomorrow!" Nate waved and turned up the walk to his front door. He turned the key and went in. The house was quiet. The family dog, Matty, was sleeping in the corner. The West Highland White Terrier was older than Nate and always seemed to be asleep.

Nate found a note from his mother on the kitchen counter.

Nate—

I will be home from work about 6:30 pm. Help yourself to some <u>healthy</u> snacks until then. We will have roasted chicken from Whole Foods for dinner.

Love you.
Mom

He reached into his backpack and pulled out the Strikers season schedule. He placed it at eye level on the refrigerator door under a large magnet for a local pizza place, then plucked a blue marker from a tall coffee mug on the counter filled with pens, pencils, and pairs of scissors.

He circled "Monarchs" and the October twenty-fourth date. "I can't wait," he whispered softly to himself.

A re you ready?" Nate's mother called from the bottom of the stairs. "Aunt Lizzie's here."

Nate tied a quick knot in his sneaker laces and bounded down the stairs.

"Hey, Lizzie. I'm ready."

His aunt stood inside the doorway talking to his mom and dad. She wore a blue soccer jersey with the number 9 on the back, white shorts, and blue kneesocks over her shin guards. Her shoulder-length reddish brown hair was pulled back in a ponytail.

"Here's my number one fan," she said as Nate jumped down the last three steps.

"When will you be back?" Nate's father asked.

"The game's at seven, so it should be over by eight-thirty," Lizzie answered. Then she added with a sly smile, "So...I should have him back by midnight."

"Very funny," Nate's mom said. "You both know it's a school night."

"But Mom, I've done all my homework," Nate protested.

"You heard what she said," his dad cautioned. "Not too late."

***

Nate climbed into the clunker of a car that Lizzie had named "Bertha." The fifteen-year-old Subaru sedan seemed to have half of Lizzie's apartment in the backseat.

"Who are you guys playing?" Nate asked.

"The Stars."

"Any good?"

"They came in second place overall last year. Maybe we can surprise them," Lizzie said, turning the key. Bertha's engine started putt-putting like an old motorboat, and one of her favorite bands blared out over the speakers.

"You still playing up front?" Nate asked.

"Oh yeah." Lizzie almost had to shout to be heard above Bertha's engine and the rock music. "I told everyone that I have to put one in the net tonight for my favorite nephew."

Nate laughed. He was Lizzie's *only* nephew. But Lizzie was the best aunt ever. Twelve years younger than Nate's mom, she seemed more like his older sister than his aunt. Lizzie had played soccer in college and now worked for a local newspaper as a reporter covering sports and politics. She took Nate to games all the time. Tonight they were headed for one of her games in a women's adult soccer league.

"We'd better hustle," Lizzie said as they pulled into a space in the high school parking lot. "I'm running a little late."

They jogged toward the lit stadium. Once they were inside, Lizzie looked over at Nate. "Come on, I'll race you!" They both took off. Nate was fast, but not as fast as his aunt. She beat him to her team's bench by a couple of steps.

"Hey, Lizzie! Nice of you to make it," a teammate called.

"I knew she'd be here," someone else said. "Lizzie would never miss a Chiefs game."

Lizzie put her arm around Nate's shoulder. "Ladies, you all remember my favorite nephew, Nate."

Suddenly Nate was in the middle of a sea of smiles.

"Look at how tall he is."

"And handsome—look at those dimples."

"What grade are you in?"

"Eighth," Nate answered. He could feel the blood rushing to his face.

"You must have a dozen girlfriends."

"I'll bet it's two dozen...at least."

"He's gonna be a heartbreaker, Lizzie."

She waved the comments aside. "He's going to be a soccer player," she declared. "Like his aunt."

As the game started, Nate climbed into the metal stands and sat near a small group of Chiefs fans. He scanned the small crowd, looking for someone he knew. Not many kids his age came to these games. Then he spotted an athletic-looking kid bouncing up the steps. *Uh-oh,* Nate thought. It was Hunter Thomas, the best player on the Monarchs. He sat across the aisle about two rows down. Not too close, but close enough. Nate slid down in his seat, hoping Hunter wouldn't see him.

But after a few minutes, Hunter called out, "Hey, Nate! What are you doing here?"

"Uh...hi. Watching my aunt. What about you?"

"My older sister's playing."

"Which team?"

"The Stars. Gold team. What about your aunt?"

"The Chiefs. Number 9."

"I guess we're always rooting for different teams." Hunter shrugged and turned his attention back to the game.

Lizzie scored the first goal on a sweet redirection of a low crossing pass. She pointed to Nate in the stands as if to say, *I told you I'd score a goal for you.*

The teams traded goals until the game was tied 3–3 late in the second half. There was still time for one more score.

Lizzie dribbled down the pitch, looking as if she wanted to win the game by herself. She leaped over a flying Stars tackler. Nate jumped out of his seat in anticipation, seeing almost nothing between Lizzie and the goal. But his aunt did not race to the net. She glanced back at the defender and slowed down, then softly kicked the ball out of bounds with her left foot.

"What the—?" Nate said out loud in the stands.

The referee blew her whistle and waved in a trainer and another Stars player from the sidelines. The defender who had missed the tackle on Lizzie lay on the ground for a moment, then got up slowly. She tested her left leg and jogged off the field, limping slightly.

The referee signaled it was the gold team's ball on the right sideline for a throw-in. The Stars fell back on defense. A Stars player threw the ball in. But instead of tossing it to a teammate, she threw it directly to Lizzie, who went back on the attack.

Nate blinked in disbelief. "I don't get it,"

he whispered under his breath. "First, Lizzie gives the ball away and then the Stars give it right back? That's weird."

Neither team was able to mount any scoring chances before the referee blew her whistle again, this time signaling the end of the game.

Nate got up and stretched.

"Good game!" Hunter called from across the way. "Your aunt's a real player."

"She played Division 1 in college," Nate said proudly.

"I can believe it." Hunter turned to walk down the steps. "See you around."

"See you on October twenty-fourth," Nate said, remembering the day of the Strikers-Monarchs game.

"Yeah, definitely."

***

Nate and Lizzie walked slowly toward the parking lot. With each step, the bright lights of the stadium melted into the darkness.

"You played great!" Nate gushed.

Lizzie smiled. "Not bad for an old lady. At least I was able to score a goal for my favorite nephew."

"By the way, what happened on that play late in the second half?" Nate asked, remembering the moment when Lizzie hadn't rushed in toward the net.

"What play?"

"The one where you blew by the defender and then slowed down and kicked the ball out of bounds."

"Oh yeah," she said. "I think the defender caught a spike and turned her ankle. The field was getting choppy."

"But you were past her," Nate said. "Why didn't you take it to the goal?"

Lizzie raised an eyebrow, looking a little annoyed. "You always stop play if you think someone is hurt."

"What do you mean?"

"It's a soccer tradition," she explained. "You're supposed to stop play if someone is down. Don't they teach you that anymore?"

"I never heard of it. They just teach us to win."

16

"Really?" Lizzie sounded surprised. "Well, I didn't want to beat the other team just because someone got hurt. Besides, they gave us the ball right back."

Nate still didn't understand. "But you had a chance to *score*," he insisted.

"Maybe. But I wouldn't want to score that way." Lizzie reached into the backseat of her car and pulled out a sweatshirt. She slipped it on to guard against the chilly autumn air.

"You want to come to the pizza place?" she asked. "Some of our players are going."

"I don't know. It *is* a school night," Nate reminded her.

Lizzie smiled her sly smile. "Don't worry. I'll have you home before midnight."

Riiiiinnng. Twenty-two notebooks snapped shut as the bell rang to end Mr. Sherman's world history class. Nate and Sergio started for the door. It was lunchtime and they were starving.

"Remember to read chapter three!" Mr. Sherman shouted above the chatter and the clatter of chairs. "You may get some questions on that material on the Friday quiz."

Nate and Sergio spilled out into the crowded corridors of Benton Middle School.

"Like your shirts," a girl said as she passed by. Nate elbowed Sergio and smiled. They were both wearing white Real Madrid team jerseys. They picked up the pace as they entered the cafeteria. The line wasn't all that long yet.

"What do you boys want?" Mrs. Bennett asked from in back of the counter.

"Meat loaf and vegetables, please," Nate answered. "Gravy on everything."

"Whoa!" Sergio stepped back as if he was shocked. "Going with the mystery meat? Brave call."

Mrs. Bennett was not amused. "What do *you* want?" she asked, staring daggers at Sergio.

"Chicken nuggets and Tater Tots," Sergio looked at Nate and whispered, "Safer choice."

"Don't be so sure. Do you know what they grind up into those nuggets?"

The two boys moved farther down the line. "I wanted to tell Mrs. Bennett 'I'll have the grease feast' but I thought she'd whack me with that big metal spoon she's holding."

Nate looked around the cafeteria and nodded toward the back. "There's Cam and Stevie, let's sit with them."

"Hey, guys," Cam said as Nate and Sergio slipped into their seats. "Cool shirts."

Sergio threw his arms back proudly to

show off the Real Madrid "Fly Emirates" emblem across his chest. "I figure we should wear championship shirts since we're going to have a championship team this season."

"Don't jinx it," Nate cautioned his teammate. "We haven't actually won a game yet. Remember?"

"Okay, okay, be Mr. Downer." Sergio motioned to Cam. "Pass the ketchup, will ya?"

Sergio squeezed the plastic ketchup bottle and a long, impolite sound echoed across the table.

"Was that you or the ketchup?" Nate teased. "I don't want you stinking up my lunch."

Sergio made a face and swirled a greasy Tater Tot in the ketchup. "How's the mystery meat?" he asked Nate.

"Not bad. You put enough gravy on anything and it tastes good."

"Heads up," Cam warned. "A couple of Monarchs at one o'clock and they're heading this way. And just look what they're wearing!"

Nate looked up and saw Hunter Thomas and Luke Jaworski walking their trays toward the four Strikers teammates. They wore the red and blue striped home jerseys of Barcelona FC, Real Madrid's biggest rival. The two Monarch players sat down at the table next to the Strikers.

"Hey, Strikers," Hunter said, glancing over at Nate and Sergio. "What are you wearing those loser shirts for?"

"Yeah," Luke chimed in. "You should get on the Barca bandwagon."

Nate spoke up. "Real Madrid's better than Barcelona any day. Madrid's got more team speed." Nate tapped his white shirt. "Like the Strikers."

"No way," Hunter said. "We're a lot faster than you guys. And Barcelona's faster than Real Madrid."

The talk bounced back and forth between the two tables as the boys debated the strengths of Real Madrid and Barcelona. The stars. The goalkeepers. The defenders. The Strikers and Monarchs knew their soccer. They could quote facts about all the games played and trophies won by the two most famous Spanish La Liga teams.

Sergio dipped another Tater Tot in his ketchup and was about to pop it in his mouth when he remembered another reason why Real Madrid was better than Barcelona.

"Yeah, well..." Before he could finish his sentence, the greasy Tater Tot slipped from his hand and rolled down the front of his Real Madrid shirt, leaving a trail of ketchup across the crisp white front like a fresh red scar.

Sergio pushed back his chair and stared at his stained shirt in horror. "Oh man, I can't believe it!" he shouted.

Everyone at the two tables burst out laughing. Some kids at another table started clapping.

"Nice hands, Sergio," Cam teased. "Good thing *you're* not the goalkeeper."

Sergio slumped in his chair, looking like someone had punched him in the gut. "I just bought this shirt," he said.

"Now what were you saying about Real

Madrid being so great?" Hunter asked.

Sergio just stared down at the shirt as if that would somehow make the stain vanish.

Nate tried to change the subject. "Who do you guys play on Saturday?" he asked Hunter.

"The Sabres."

"You'll beat them...easy."

"I don't know, they're pretty good. They've got J. J. Locke. He can score. What about you guys?"

"We play the Sharks at noon."

"You should beat them." He paused and looked at Sergio's shirt. "Unless Sergio spills ketchup all over your team."

Sergio barely lifted his head.

"Forget about the shirt," Nate said. "Your mom will wash it."

This didn't make Sergio any happier. "I still have to go through the rest of the day wearing my lunch. I'll look like a clumsy doofus."

"Why don't you turn the shirt inside out?" Cam suggested.

Sergio wasn't buying. "Yeah, right," he

said. "So I'll look like a complete dork? Like I get dressed in the dark or something?"

Nate, Cam, and Stevie got up from the table with their trays. "Those are your choices," Nate said. "Doofus or dork. What'll it be?"

Sergio got up very slowly, still staring at the brand-new, stained shirt in disbelief.

"Doofus," he sighed.

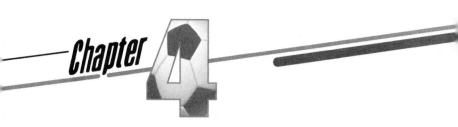
Nate and Sergio jogged slowly through the honeycomb of soccer fields at the SoccerPlex.

"Did you find out what happened in the Monarchs game this morning?" Sergio asked.

"They won, 3–0," Nate said, still running. "Looks like J. J. Locke wasn't such a great scorer after all."

"I guess we better win today too."

Coach Lyn called the team together for pregame instructions. "All right, guys. First game. Let's get off to a really good start. Remember, pass the ball. One, maybe two touches and then get rid of it. Midfielders, look for Nate and Anton upfield. Nate, when you get the ball, take it to the Sharks goal. Be aggressive. Let's put some pressure on them."

Nate bounced up and down on the balls of his feet as Coach Lyn spoke. He pumped his legs as if running in place. He could hardly wait for the opening whistle.

As he walked onto the soccer pitch, he spied his mother, father, and aunt on the sidelines. Lizzie put two fingers in her mouth and let loose a long, loud whistle.

"Let's go, Strikers!" she shouted.

The teams got off to a slow start and made a lot of nervous, sloppy passes. Nate spent most of his time jogging up and down the field hoping for something to happen. Another pass by Sergio missed its mark. *He's probably still worrying about his Real Madrid shirt,* Nate thought.

Finally Sergio intercepted a pass and Nate sensed a chance. He raced down the right sideline. After a couple of quick dribbles, Sergio slipped him a perfect pass. Nate gained control with a quick touch and saw Sergio running straight down the middle of the field, still chasing the play.

In two steps, Nate was dribbling at top speed toward the corner. His hustle caught the defense by surprise and gave him enough space to spin a crossing pass toward the space about fifteen yards in front of the goal.

The Sharks goalkeeper came out, but it was too late. Nate's pass curled away from the keeper's outstretched hands and found its mark. Sergio left-footed the ball into the back of the net.

Goal!

Sergio ran around the field in a crazy figure eight, grinning. His arms were spread wide like a human airplane. The Strikers had their first goal of the season and were ahead 1–0!

Minutes later, a long pass found Nate along the sideline again. This time he broke for the middle of the field, stepped by a defender, and with a couple of stutter-step dribbles set up a powerful right-footed shot.

Boom! The ball swerved past the diving goalkeeper and found the corner of the net.

Goal!

Now it was Nate's turn to run around with his arms outstretched. Sergio and the other Strikers encircled him, pounding his back and shoulders in congratulations.

When Nate emerged from the happy circle, he saw his parents and Aunt Lizzie jumping up and down and cheering on the sidelines.

"All right!"

"Way to go, Nate the Great!"

"Go, Strikers!"

At halftime, Nate and Sergio sat on the grass gulping water and sucking orange slices.

Sergio lay back and stared up at the sky. "We've got this one," he said confidently.

Nate looked out across the pitch. "The Monarchs won their game 3–0," he said. "It would be cool if we could do the same. Let's keep the pressure on."

The Strikers kept the pressure on but couldn't get the third goal. Nate whistled a couple of shots above the crossbar. The Sharks goalkeeper robbed Sergio of a goal with a stretched-out, diving save. Another shot by Anton Draves, the other Strikers forward, rattled the post and bounced away.

With just a few minutes left in the game, the Sharks counterattacked. Some confident passes found a Sharks forward open near the top of the penalty area. Caught by surprise, the Strikers defense was out of position. The forward blasted a shot after barely looking at the goal. The ball spun past a surprised Cam and into the upper corner of the net.

Goal!

The score was 2–1. The Strikers were in a real game.

"Come on, tighten up the defense!" Coach Lyn called, clapping his hands. "Forwards, fall back on defense. And don't take any chances."

The Strikers followed orders. They forgot about scoring another goal and concentrated on keeping the Sharks away from the goal. They were now hoping to hold on for a win.

Nate let out a big sigh of relief when the

referee blew his whistle and crossed his hands over his head to signal the end of the game.

The Strikers had squeaked by, 2–1.

Nate's mom, dad, and aunt were all smiles when they walked up to Nate after the game.

"Good start," Dad said.

"Nice goal," Lizzie added.

Nate laughed. "I figured you scored one for me the other night. I wanted to return the favor."

"Are you two competing to see who can score the most goals this season?" Nate's mom asked.

Lizzie's eyes lit up. "I'm game," she said. "Family goal-scoring championship. What do you say?"

Nate thought for a moment. "Okay, but what does the winner get?"

"How about the loser has to make cookies for the winner?" Lizzie suggested.

"You've got a bet." The two shook hands.

Nate's mother put her arm around him.

"You know, I think I may have to root for my kid sister."

"What are you talking about?" Nate said. "You want your own son to lose a bet?"

She pulled Nate closer. "No, but I would love to see my own son making cookies."

Chapter 5

Coach Roland, the gym teacher at Benson Middle School, poked his head into the boys' locker room. "Hurry up, guys!" he shouted. "Mile run today."

Most of the boys groaned. But Nate tugged the laces of his sneakers tight, then pulled a Benson Middle School sweatshirt over his head.

"Hey, Nate!" Hunter Thomas called across the noisy locker room. "Is Sergio here?"

Nate looked down the row of lockers and saw Sergio tossing his school shoes in a locker.

"Yeah, why?"

"Anybody else here from the Strikers?" Hunter asked.

Nate looked around and saw Cameron and Stevie. "Yeah, we've got four guys."

"Perfect."

"What's up?"

"I'll tell you when we get outside," Hunter answered.

***

The class was jogging around the track in the misty morning sunshine to warm up when Hunter pulled alongside Nate.

"Remember how you said you guys were faster than us? We've got four guys from the Monarchs in class," he said. "And you've got four guys from the Strikers. How 'bout we make it a race?"

"How?" Sergio interrupted.

"Simple. Coach Roland is going to keep the times for the mile run. We'll just add up the four times and—"

"The team with the lowest total time wins," Luke Jaworski said, finishing his teammate's thought.

Nate did a quick rundown in his head of

the two teams. *I'm the fastest, but I'm not sure I can beat Hunter in a mile race. Sergio's fast too, but Luke and Taj Oquendo are pretty good. Stevie's not that fast, but he can run all day. That should help in a mile. I don't know about Cam. Goalkeepers don't have to run much. But maybe he can beat Mikael Sukorov.*

"All right," Nate said finally. "But what do the winners get?"

"I don't know," Hunter said. He slowed down as if to think about it. "Let's say losers have to buy each of the winners an ice cream sandwich at lunch today."

Nate looked around at Sergio, Cam, and Stevie. Sergio gave Nate a quick nod.

"Okay, you're on," Nate said. "Strikers against the Monarchs."

After the warm-up, Coach Roland gathered the class at the center of the track and explained how the mile would be run and timed. "It's four times around the track. We've got thirty-six kids in class, so we'll run in three groups of twelve. When the first group of twelve is running, each person in the second group will be keeping time for an assigned runner. The third group will time the second group's runs, then the first group will keep track of the third group's times. I'll post the times outside the locker room at the end of class. Okay, line up!"

Hunter grabbed Nate by the arm. "Let's line up all our guys in the back so we can run in the last group." Nate gave Sergio, Cam, and Stevie the word and the boys moved to the back of the line.

"All right, first twelve!" Coach Roland shouted.

As soon as that group took off, Nate and the other Strikers huddled together.

"So what's our strategy going to be?" Nate asked.

Sergio seemed confused. "What do you mean? We just run."

"If we want to beat those guys," Nate explained, "we all have to run our best races."

"Nate's right," Cam agreed. "We've got to run smart."

Nate decided to take charge. "Listen, I'm

the fastest, so why don't I set the pace? We'll run as a group. I'll run at a comfortable speed, 75 or 80 percent, for the first two and a half laps. Then I'll try to really step it up."

"Yeah," Sergio agreed. "If the rest of us can keep up the pace, great. If not, we'll still probably have a decent time."

The first group finished their run, and the Strikers each took a stopwatch and lined up across from a runner in the second group. Coach Roland called out, "All right, second twelve get ready!"

When the runners were in place, the coach shouted, "Ready! Set!" and then blew his whistle.

As the last boys from the second group straggled across the finish line, the Strikers and the Monarchs gave the times to Coach Roland and handed their stopwatches to a classmate.

"Everybody know who you're timing? Okay, third group get ready."

Nate shook his legs to get warm. He rolled his shoulders and swiveled his neck from side to side. The twelve runners toed the starting line.

"On your mark!" Coach Roland called out. "Get set! Go!"

The four Strikers stuck to their strategy. They took off in a tight diamond-shaped pack: Nate in the lead setting the pace, with Sergio and Stevie at his shoulders and Cam following close behind. The Monarchs ran in a similar formation just a step or two behind the Strikers.

The two groups ran around the track once...twice...staying tightly bunched as the other four runners trailed far behind. Early in the third lap, Hunter and Luke broke away from their teammates and bolted ahead of the Strikers.

Nate and his teammates didn't panic. They stuck together until the halfway point of the third lap. Then, as planned, Nate stepped up the pace. He concentrated on Hunter's and Luke's backs as if they had targets on them. Nate was creeping up slowly but steadily when Coach Roland shouted out, "One lap to go!"

Nate took a quick glance over his shoulder as he rounded the first turn. The runners were stretching out now, with the second group about fifteen or twenty yards behind the leaders.

I've got to win this group, Nate thought and flipped it into another gear. He passed Luke on the backstretch and set his sights on Hunter just a few yards ahead.

Hunter stayed on the inside on the last turn, forcing Nate to the outside. Nate ran at Hunter's right shoulder, and he could hear him breathing and their racing feet slapping against the track.

As they turned into the homestretch, Nate and Hunter were matching each other step for step. Nate pulled out one final burst of energy to surge ahead with only twenty yards to go. He flashed across the finish line just two steps ahead of Hunter.

Luke followed in third just a couple of steps ahead of Sergio. Then came Stevie, the two Monarchs, and finally Cam, still racing hard at the end.

The runners bent over near the finish line, gasping for breath. *It's going to be close,* Nate thought.

The timekeepers circled Coach Roland,

who wrote down the times. "Get ready for your next class!" he called out. "I'll post the times. Real good job by the last group, by the way. You guys had some great times."

The locker room filled with good-natured kidding as the boys dressed for their next class.

"We definitely beat you guys."

"No way. I can almost taste that ice cream sandwich right now."

"No wonder Cam plays goal. He's a slow-poke."

"Keepers got to be quick," Cam said in his defense. "Not fast."

After they got dressed, the boys bunched around the long list of names and times posted on the wall. Sergio pulled out his phone. First he typed in the times for Nate, Sergio, Stevie, and Cam. Then he started on the Monarchs. Nate could see Luke doing the same thing.

"I don't believe it!" Sergio cried out as he clicked in the last number.

"What?"

"We tied."

"You're kidding," Nate said. "Let me see the numbers."

"That's what I got too," Luke said as he handed his calculations to Hunter.

Nate studied the numbers on Sergio's screen.

Nate	5:34	Hunter	5:36
Sergio	5:46	Luke	5:42
Stevie	5:53	Taj	5:59
Cam	6:15	Mikael	6:11
Total:	23:28		23:28

Nate looked straight up in disbelief. "If we'd been one second faster, we would've beat them."

Sergio shrugged. With a click, the numbers disappeared from the screen.

Nate's shoulders sank. "I really wanted to beat them," he said to no one in particular.

Sergio put a sympathetic arm around his friend's shoulder. "To tell you the truth, I really wanted the ice cream sandwich."

Chapter 6

Come on, get me the ball, Nate thought as he jogged back and forth near midfield. He checked the scoreboard.

STRIKERS		VIPERS
0	7:05 HALF 2	0

They were still tied 0–0. Much of the game had been played in the Strikers end with the Vipers pressing the attack. Nate was getting impatient with the lack of a Strikers offense. It was as if he had hardly been in the game. His game shirt wasn't even sweaty.

The Vipers right forward sailed a dangerous crossing pass toward the front of the Strikers net. Nate instinctively took a few steps closer to the right sideline.

Cam was ready. He stepped out and with a quick leap snatched the ball out of the sky. But instead of waiting for his teammates to run downfield, Cam whipped a long sidearm bounce pass down the right sideline.

Nate and a Vipers defender raced toward the ball. Nate beat him to it, stopped on a dime, and with a slick heel kick flicked the ball back toward the Vipers goal as the defender flashed by. Nate now had nothing but open field between him and the Vipers' goal!

The Vipers defender skidded to a stop and scrambled to catch up. Nate pushed the ball ahead of him, sprinting to the Vipers goal. Finally he had a chance to score.

Another defender dashed over to cut Nate off. But Nate was really flying now, a game's worth of stored-up energy bursting out of him. He cut sharply to the left, leaving another Viper defender in his dust. With a light touch, Nate was in the clear and bearing down on the goal.

Breakaway!

The Vipers goalkeeper dashed out, hoping to grab the ball before Nate's next touch. Nate tapped the ball to the right just as the keeper tumbled forward, grabbing nothing but grass and air. Nate leaped over the diving keeper and sprinted to the ball, now bouncing toward the goal line. He reached out with his right foot and redirected the ball toward the open net. The net jumped back.

Goal! The Strikers were ahead, 1–0.

Nate sprang into the air and spun around, then raced back into his shouting teammates' arms.

"All right, breakaway!"

"Great goal!"

"Super move."

"We finally got you the ball!" Sergio shouted.

"What do you mean 'we'?" Nate laughed. "Cam got me the ball. What a pass." He pointed the index fingers of both hands down the field to the Strikers keeper.

Cam raised a gloved fist.

Coach Lyn paced the sidelines, clapping his hands. "All right! Good defense! Nate and Anton, drop back and help out. We've got to keep the lead."

The Strikers played carefully for the last few minutes, milking the clock with each possession. The forwards fell back, packing the defensive end and jamming play in the middle of the field.

Nate didn't have any more scoring chances, but neither did the Vipers. When the referee blew the whistle to end the game, Nate jabbed his fist into the air.

The Strikers had won again, 1–0.

After shaking hands with the Vipers, Nate and his teammates turned toward the bench.

"Hey, look," Nate said scanning the sidelines. "It's some of the Monarchs—I see Hunter and Luke."

"Yeah, I saw them," Sergio said. "They were watching the game."

"I'll bet they were rooting for a tie," Stevie said.

"Or a loss," Nate added.

"What were you watching the sidelines for?" Cam asked in mock outrage. "Next time, pay attention to the game. They must have had a million shots on me today."

Sergio held his arms out to his sides. "Hey, I'm just saying I saw them."

"Hunter!" Nate shouted. "How'd you guys do today?"

"We won. Easy, 4–0."

"Who'd you play?"

"The Rapids."

"They stink!" Sergio shouted. "We'll beat them 6–0."

Nate lowered his voice. "The Rapids aren't *that* bad. The Monarchs must be playing really well to win 4–0."

"We've got a few more weeks before we play the Monarchs," Sergio said. "We'll be ready."

"Yeah, if you pay attention to the game and stop checking out who's in the crowd," Cam teased.

Nate traded high fives with his father and mother, who were waiting near the parking lot. Aunt Lizzie was all smiles. "Great goal," she said. "You were really motoring on that breakaway."

Nate held up two fingers. "I got two goals in two games. You'd better start looking up cookie recipes."

"Or I'd better score another goal this weekend to catch up." She looked at Nate as if she'd just remembered something. "Hey, I'm covering the Saint Joe's–Landis Prep football game tonight. You want to come? I might be able to sneak you into the press box."

Nate looked at his mother and father with big, begging eyes. "Can I?"

"I don't see why not," his mother said. "It's not a school night."

Nate's father laughed. "But you'll still have him home by midnight. Right, Lizzie?"

Aunt Lizzie gave him an angelic look and posed her hands like she was swearing on a bible in a courtroom.

"I do solemnly promise," she said.

Chapter 7

Nate and Aunt Lizzie climbed the concrete steps to the press box perched at the top of the Landis Prep stadium. Lizzie opened the door. A long, flat wooden table sat in front of three windows. Ten metal folding chairs were scattered along the length of the table.

"Hey, Tom!" Lizzie called to an older man in front of a laptop.

The man took a sip from his Styrofoam cup without looking up. "Hi, Lizzie. What's up?" Then he noticed Nate. "Your paper's paying for assistants now?"

"Yeah, right," Lizzie said. "This is my favorite nephew, Nate. He's going to hang out here and watch the game. Is that okay?"

"No problem," Tom said. He eyed Nate. "You play football?" he asked.

"No sir, I play soccer."

"He scored the winning goal in his game today," Lizzie said proudly. "On a breakaway."

Tom nodded. He looked tired even though it wasn't even seven o'clock. "You like football?" Tom asked.

"Sure."

Tom brightened. "Good. Then you're in for a treat. Saint Joe's and Landis Prep are big rivals. They have two of the best football programs in the area."

"Who are you rooting for?" Nate asked.

Lizzie interrupted quickly. "First rule up here in the press box: we don't root for any team." She turned to Tom. "No cheering in the press box. Right, Tom?"

Tom nodded and took another sip of coffee. "We root for the best story," he said with a hint of a smile.

"When was the last time Saint Joe's beat Landis?" Lizzie asked.

Tom thought for a moment. "About ten

years ago," he said. "But the games are always close. They go right down to the wire. Last year Landis won on the last play of the game."

"We'll root for Saint Joe's," Lizzie whispered to Nate. "It's a better story if they win."

Lizzie opened her laptop and started typing. A few more reporters wandered in and sat down. The stands were filling up fast. Soon people packed every corner of the stadium. Even sitting way up in the press box, Nate could feel the hum of excitement in the crowd.

The moment the game started, it was all business among the reporters. Just as Lizzie had said, there was no cheering. They typed away, occasionally tossing comments or questions at another reporter.

"What's the running back's name?"

"Which one?"

"Number 24. The kid from Landis."

"Jarvis LaChance."

"Isn't he the kid who's going to the University of Virginia next year?"

"Yeah."

"He can play."

Nate sat quietly. Finally, during a time-out, he asked Lizzie, "What are you typing?"

"A running description of the game," she said, keeping her eyes fixed on the field. "I'll put the final score and a quick summary of the game in the first paragraph, the one we call the 'lede.' The game stuff will go in the back."

Landis Prep jumped out to a 14–0 lead behind a powerful running attack led by LaChance. But Saint Joe's didn't give up. They scored a touchdown before the end of the first half, then scored again in the second half on a wild, broken-field 72-yard run. The score was tied, 14–14.

Landis Prep put together a long drive, eating up yards and the clock. They scored on a short pass and regained the lead, 21–14.

Saint Joe's came back again. Starting with only three minutes to go, they drove downfield until it was fourth down on the eight-yard line with just twenty seconds to go. Everyone in the stadium was on their feet. The Saint Joe's quarterback faded back but couldn't find an open receiver. He scrambled to his right and fired a desperation pass to the back corner of the end zone. The Saint Joe's receiver stretched out, snagged the ball, touched the chalk sideline, and tumbled out of bounds. The linesman raced in, pulling both hands toward his chest.

"Touchdown!" Nate shouted. He couldn't help cheering. Suddenly the press box was alive and full of talk.

"Score's 21–20. Think they'll go for two points?"

"The St. Joe's coach may want at least a tie. After all, they've lost ten in a row."

"There's no overtime. They'll go for it."

"Five bucks says they go for two."

Nobody took the bet. Saint Joe's was already lining up for the two-point conversion. The quarterback pitched the ball back to the running back, who was sweeping around the right end. A Landis Prep defensive back sliced through the line and tripped up the running back just short of the goal line.

The Landis Prep side exploded in cheers. The Saint Joe's fans groaned as the runner slammed the ball into the turf—one yard short of victory.

"Watch my laptop," Lizzie ordered Nate as the fans spilled onto the field. "I've got to get some quotes." She grabbed a notebook and was out the door.

"I told you it'd be a great game." Tom leaned back in his chair and shook his head. "And boy, that was the best game I've seen in a long time."

When Lizzie returned, she sat down with her notebook and started typing again. After a few minutes she sat forward with her chin in her hands and silently read the article. She made a few final changes and hit the send button.

"All done," Lizzie said with a satisfied smile. "Pretty good game, huh?"

"Yeah, but I'll bet the Saint Joe's guys are mad," Nate said.

Lizzie started to collect her things. "Yeah,

they have to be disappointed," she agreed. "But I think in a couple of days they'll be okay."

Nate wasn't buying that. "But they lost to a big rival...again!" he said, thinking of how he would feel if the Strikers lost to the Monarchs. "I'd be *real* disappointed."

"I don't know," Lizzie said as they stepped out of the press box and into the nearly empty stadium. "I think they'll see they played a great game—maybe one of their best—against a terrific opponent. They just came up a little short. That's all."

"Yeah, but..."

"Who's your big rival?"

"The Monarchs."

"Right, the Monarchs," Lizzie said. They were walking across the football field under the lights, surrounded by the night and the quiet. "You always have a great game against them, right?"

"Yeah, but..."

"You remember all those games, don't you? The Monarchs bring out the best in you guys. And you guys bring out the best in the Monarchs. You want to beat 'em, but if give it your very best shot, everything you've got, and then lose fair and square? That's not the worst thing in the world, is it?"

"I guess not," Nate said. "But I'd still want to win."

"It's like that thing about kicking the ball out of bounds," Lizzie continued. "You want to win, but you want to win the right way. Straight up. Not because someone got hurt."

Nate walked across the field, with everything Lizzie had talked about—Saint Joe's and Landis Prep, winning and losing, giving it your best, kicking the ball out of bounds after an injury—bouncing around in his mind like so many soccer balls.

He understood what his aunt was trying to tell him. But a big part of him still wanted the Strikers to beat the Monarchs. Any way they could.

Chapter 8

Nate heard someone call his name and turned to see Ben Goodwin, a Strikers substitute, jogging onto the pitch. Nate didn't want to leave the game, but he saw Coach Lyn waving him to the sidelines.

"I wanted to give you a quick break," the coach explained. "You've been doing a lot of running. I'll get you back in the game in a couple of minutes." He clapped Nate on the back. "We're going to need you."

Nate found his water bottle and squirted a steady stream of water into his mouth. He grabbed a couple of orange slices and sucked on them, letting the juice dribble down his chin as he checked the scoreboard.

STRIKERS   **UNITED**

2   8:00 HALF 2   3

The Strikers were behind 3–2 with only eight minutes to go. Nate replayed the game in his head up to this point. The Strikers had jumped off to an early lead, but the United had come right back to tie the score 1–1. Nate smiled as he remembered the goal that had put the Strikers ahead 2–1. Sergio had slipped a sweet pass to Nate near the top of the penalty box. Nate had wasted no time and blasted a rocket into the back of the net.

But not long after that, the Strikers defense broke down and gave up a pair of unanswered goals. So now the Strikers were in real trouble. Nate stood with his hands on his hips, breathing deeply, trying to get ready for one last big push.

"Nate, go in for Ben."

Nate sprinted on to the field thinking, I'd better make something happen...*quickly.*

He scrambled after the ball, but the United defender flicked it to a teammate and started to play keep-away. Nate could feel the game clock running down.

Sergio intercepted a pass near midfield. He sent a quick pass to Nate, who was racing along the right wing.

This may be our last chance, Nate told himself. He glanced over and saw Sergio still running down the middle of the field.

Nate dribbled down the sideline, aiming for the corner. He faked toward the middle, freezing the closest United defender and creating enough space so he could loft a high centering pass toward Sergio near the front of the United goal.

The pass felt good as it left Nate's right foot. Maybe too good. The ball sailed past the sprinting Sergio and the United goalkeeper and found Anton, the other Strikers forward near the far post, who volleyed the ball into the back of the net.

Goal! The game was tied 3–3.

The Strikers players erupted into cheers. "All tied up!"

"Great goal, Anton!"

"Way to pass, Nate!"

Nate tried to settle everyone quickly. "Come on, guys, we still have some time. We need another goal. We need a win!"

The Strikers had time, but not enough. A couple of minutes later, the referee blew his whistle to end the game. The Strikers and the United had tied.

"At least we got a tie," Sergio said as the boys collected their equipment and water bottles from the sidelines. "That's a point in the standings."

"Yeah, but a win is three points," Nate said. "We're going to need every point we can get to stay with the Monarchs."

Cam's head dropped. "I never should've let in three goals," he said as he tossed his goalkeeper gloves into his athletic bag.

"It wasn't just you," Nate argued. "The rest of us didn't play that great either. We've got to start playing better soon—we play the Monarchs in four weeks."

The boys fell silent. They were still disappointed with the 3–3 tie.

"There's nothing we can do about it now," Nate said.

"There is *something* we can do about it," Sergio suggested.

"Like what?" Cam asked. "Have one of the United goals taken back on instant replay or something? This isn't the NFL, you know."

Sergio smiled. "No. We can root like crazy *against* the Monarchs. We need any kind of help we can get."

He scanned the fields at the SoccerPlex. Kids of all ages were playing games in the bright September sun. Parents and fans stood on the edges of the fields and sat on small metal bleachers.

"I think the Monarchs are playing over there," Sergio said, pointing toward a field on the other side of the complex.

"Let's go," Cam said. He and Sergio lead the way, weaving through the fans on the sidelines, and Nate trailed behind. When they reached the field where their rivals were playing, Nate checked the scoreboard. The Monarchs were leading 2–0.

"How's the game been?" Nate asked a parent standing nearby.

"The Monarchs are really good. They've been controlling play most of the game. They're beating us 2–0."

The Sabres parent noticed Nate's uniform. "Which team are you on?" he asked.

"The Strikers."

"I think we play you in a couple of weeks," he said. "How'd you do today?"

"We tied the United, 3–3."

The ball whistled by the Monarchs goal. The parent threw his hands in the air. "Oooohhhh," he groaned. "We really needed that goal."

Nate and his teammates moved in so they could see better.

Sergio and Cam cheered loudly.

"Comeback time!"

"Let's go, Sabres!"

"Keep fighting, you can do it!"

Nate held his hand over his forehead to block the sun, the sweat drying on his arms and face. He stood and watched the game in silence as the action flowed back and forth across the pitch.

It doesn't seem right to root for the Monarchs to lose, he thought. *Maybe Aunt Lizzie's right. The best thing would be to beat the Monarchs when they're playing their best. Straight up. No injuries. No lucky breaks. The right way.*

The Monarchs pressed the attack on the Sabres goal with a series of pinpoint passes. Hunter curved a shot around the Sabres goalkeeper for another goal.

Nate watched as the Monarchs celebrated. *But I sure can't cheer for a Monarch victory,* he said to himself. *I just hope we can beat them.*

Nate turned the key to the front door and stepped inside with Sergio. The house was quiet. There were no lights except for the afternoon October sun streaming in the windows.

Sergio pointed to Matty, the West Highland Terrier snoring softly on the dog bed in the corner. "Man, that dog is always asleep."

"He doesn't sleep that much," Nate said, defending his dog.

"Are you kidding?" Sergio exclaimed. "I'm over at your house all the time and I never see him awake."

"He wakes up," Nate said. "To go pee and poop in the backyard."

Sergio made a face. "Remind me never to play in your backyard."

"Anyway, give him a break," Nate said. "He's old."

"How old?"

"We're not sure. We got him from a rescue league. But he's about fifteen years old. Maybe sixteen."

Sergio did the math in his head. "If you figure seven dog years for every human year, he's...105!"

"Or 112."

"You're right," Sergio agreed. "He's old. Let him sleep."

"Come on." Nate headed toward the stairs. "Let's check out the league website."

"Again?"

"Come on."

The two boys sprinted up the steps, with Nate taking them two at a time. They tossed their backpacks on Nate's bed. Nate turned on the laptop on his desk, tapped a few keys, and stared at the screen. When the website came up, he clicked on the icon labeled "League Standings."

Team	Record [W–L–T]	Points
Monarchs	6–0–0	18
Strikers	5–0–1	16
Devils	5–1–0	15
United	3–2–1	10
Rush	3–3–0	9
Sabres	2–2–2	8
Vipers	2–3–1	7
Barracudas	1–4–1	3
Sharks	0–6–0	0
Rapids	0–6–0	0

Nate and Sergio studied the numbers. The Strikers were two points behind the Monarchs.

"That tie really hurt us," Nate said, stating the obvious.

"We're still undefeated," Sergio protested.

"So are the Monarchs. And they don't have a tie. That's why this week's game against them is so important. If we lose, there's no way we can catch them."

Nate clicked on another heading and the league's schedule of games appeared on the screen.

"The Monarchs play the Devils on the last week of the season," Nate declared.

"Maybe the Monarchs will lose that game."

Sergio shook his head. "No way. The Monarchs will win against them."

"Don't be too sure," Nate said. "The Devils are pretty good. Remember, we were lucky to beat them back in early October. And they've gotten better."

Sergio nudged Nate's arm and pointed at the keyboard. "How are you doing in the goal-scoring race? Look it up."

Nate's fingers danced across the keyboard. Another row of names and numbers appeared on the screen.

Name	Team	Goals
Sean McCarthy	Devils	8
Nate Osborne	Strikers	6
Hunter Thomas	Monarchs	6
J. J. Locke	Sabres	6
Tyler Westgate	United	5

"How did Sean McCarthy get in front?" Sergio asked.

"I think he scored three goals against the Rapids."

"You're kidding!" Sergio said. "Their defense wasn't that bad. How many goals did you score against them?"

"One."

"One? Why didn't you score more?"

Nate pointed an accusing finger at Sergio. "Because *you* didn't get me the ball," he teased. "You're always hogging it." Before his friend could defend himself, Nate added, "But it doesn't matter because I'm still ahead in the big scoring race."

"What are you talking about?

"I've got a bet with my Aunt Lizzie," Nate explained. "Whoever scores the most goals wins. Right now, I've got six goals and Lizzie has five. So I'm one goal ahead in our bet."

"What do you get if you win?"

A big grin spread across Nate's face. "Cookies," he said. "Homemade chocolate chip cookies. So you've got to get me the ball."

"If I do," Sergio said. "Do I get some of the cookies?"

"Sure, I'll give you some. But you have to pass me the ball."

Sergio's face lit up. "For homemade cookies? I'm definitely passing you the ball. All day long!"

Chapter 10

A cool autumn wind swept across the SoccerPlex. Nate and Sergio bounced up and down on the sidelines trying to stay warm. They were too excited to stand still anyway.

The game with the Monarchs was finally here.

"Bring it in!" Coach Lyn shouted.

The Strikers huddled close around their coach for their final instructions. "I don't have to tell you this is a big game." He looked around at the players. "Stevie, you have to mark Hunter Thomas. Stay close to him. Don't give him room to operate. Sergio, you and the other midfielders have to drop back and help on defense. Nate, be aggressive.

You have to test their defense. If you get a chance to shoot, take it."

The coach reached his hand out. One by one the team members put their hands on top of his. Nate could feel the growing anticipation in the tight circle.

"We've waited all year for this game," Coach Lyn said. "Give it everything you've got." He paused and the entire team chanted, "One…two…three…hustle!"

The Strikers *had* to hustle, because the Monarchs were good. Very good. During the first few minutes, they moved the ball crisply from player to player until Hunter ripped off a first shot. Stevie was just close enough to the Monarchs' star forward that he couldn't get a clear shot on net, and the ball flew wide of the goal.

"All right!" Cam shouted, making a fist with his goalkeeper gloves. "Good play, defense. Way to go, Stevie!"

The game settled into a defensive struggle. Every ball was a battle. Nate barely had room to breathe because the Monarchs' best defender, Luke Jaworski, was marking him like a shadow. Nate couldn't shake him. He felt a hand or elbow on him almost anywhere he went.

The first half ended in a scoreless tie. "A tie hurts us a lot more than it hurts them," Nate said, thinking back to the league standings.

"Then we'd better win," Sergio said.

The second half was more middle field play and tight defense. Nate drifted on the edge of the action, getting frustrated at the lack of scoring chances.

Then a ball floated down the middle into the Monarchs' half of the field. Nate, Sergio, and two Monarch defenders converged on the play, positioning themselves for a header.

Sergio's taller than me, Nate thought as he approached the clutch of players. *He's got a better chance to win the ball.* So Nate didn't jump with the others. Instead, he spun toward the Monarchs goal.

His bet paid off. Sergio won the midair fight and headed the ball to Nate, who controlled it with one quick touch.

I don't have much time, he thought as he raced downfield. *The Monarchs defense is already after me. I'd better kick it hard and hope it's on goal.*

Nate brought back his right foot and fired a hard shot toward the far post. The ball curved around the keeper, glanced off the inside of the post, and tucked into the corner of the net.

Goal! The Strikers led 1–0.

As the Strikers celebrated, Nate reminded them the game wasn't over. Not by a long shot. "There's plenty of time left!" he shouted. "We've got to play tight D!"

The Monarchs were now on full attack, no holding back. They were desperate to tie the game. Their passes were quick and left the Strikers defense scrambling to catch up.

With about ten minutes left in the game, a Monarchs midfielder slipped a pass to Hunter, who was racing through a crack in the Strikers defense. Hunter squeezed past Stevie and chipped a soft shot over Cameron's diving attempt at a save. The ball bounced into the goal.

Just like that, the score was tied, 1–1.

Nate could feel the energy seeping out of his teammates. "Come on, Strikers!" he yelled. "We've still got time. We can win this game!"

The Monarchs tightened their defense. Hunter and his teammates looked like they were happy to play for a tie.

We can't settle for a tie, Nate thought as he patrolled midfield. *If I get an opening, I've got to be aggressive. We have to gain three points in the standings—not just one.*

With a couple of minutes left in the game, a long pass found Nate and Luke jockeying for position. Nate controlled the ball with his chest about twenty-five yards away from the Monarchs goal. Luke was still marking him closely. Nate could feel his hand on his back.

Nate faked left and spun right, hoping to lose Luke and head to the goal. As he spun free, Nate heard a strange cracking sound, almost like the snapping of a twig.

Unnhh! Luke groaned and fell away.

Suddenly Nate was in open space with a clear path to the goal and a chance to win the game!

But he glanced back and saw Luke crumpled on the pitch, reaching for his right ankle. The referee, who was far away from the play, had not blown his whistle. Still, Nate heard his Aunt Lizzie's voice in his head. "You want to win, but you want to win the right way. Not because someone got hurt."

Almost without thinking, Nate took two quick steps and left-footed the ball across the right sideline. Out of bounds.

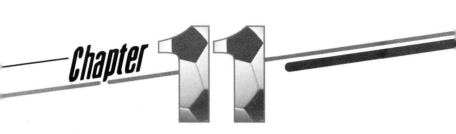

Chapter 11

Sergio, who was rushing down the center of the field hoping for a crossing pass, stopped dead in his tracks.

"What are you doing?" he shouted at Nate, his arms spread wide.

Nate circled back to Luke, who was still on the ground holding his ankle. "He's hurt," Nate explained.

"So...so what?" Sergio sputtered with his fists clenched at his side. "The ref didn't blow the whistle."

Luke rolled over on his back, and the referee finally ran up and crossed his hands over his head. He blew his whistle and shouted, "My time!"

The Monarchs coach jogged onto the field

and helped Luke to the sidelines. The defender was still favoring his right ankle. A Monarchs substitute ran onto the pitch.

Nate and Sergio stood off to the side as the referee signaled that it was Monarchs ball on a throw-in.

"We don't even get the ball," Sergio said, gritting his teeth.

"They'll give it right back," Nate replied.

"Says who?"

"They're supposed to."

Sergio shook his head. "You had a chance to go for the goal...or pass it to me. I was wide open. We could have scored. We could have beat these guys."

Nate looked at Luke standing on one foot on the Monarchs sideline. "I didn't want to score with him lying on the ground. I mean...that doesn't seem right."

"Play the whistle," Sergio said. "We've been taught that ever since U-6 soccer. Remember? Anyway, do you think any of the Monarchs would have kicked the ball out of bounds just because one of us might have been hurt?"

Nate wasn't 100 percent sure of the answer to that question.

The referee blew his whistle to resume play. To Nate's surprise, the Monarchs didn't pass the ball in to the Strikers. Instead, they passed the ball in to a defender, who boomed a long kick out of the Monarchs end.

Sergio shot Nate a disgusted look as the two players chased the action downfield.

Nate felt confused. *I thought for sure Lizzie would know what she was talking about after that game,* he thought as he raced down the field. The two teams continued to battle over every possession. Not only did the Monarchs not give the Strikers the ball, they gave the Strikers nothing. The Monarchs were playing just as hard as in the beginning of the game.

This isn't turning out the way Aunt Lizzie said it would, Nate thought.

Finally the whistle blew. The Strikers and the Monarchs had tied, 1–1. But looking at the two teams, anyone would have thought the Monarchs had won and the

Strikers had lost. The Monarchs traded high fives while the Strikers drifted over to their bench.

"Another tie," Sergio growled as he slammed his equipment into his gym bag. "When are we going to beat those guys?"

"We'll beat them in the championship game," Nate said, trying to convince himself.

"If we *make* the championship game." Sergio swung his equipment bag over his shoulder. "By the way, I thought you said they were going to give us the ball back."

Nate could hear the anger in Sergio's voice. "They were supposed to," Nate said.

"Well, they didn't. Who said they would?"

"My Aunt Liz. She played in college, remember?"

Sergio's face twisted into a scowl. "Is this some sort of girls' rule or something?"

"No." Nate could feel his face getting warm. "It's not really a rule, it's...it's...just the way you're supposed to play. You don't want to win just because someone got hurt. At least that's what Lizzie said."

"Well, whatever it is, it didn't work out so great for us." Sergio turned and walked away. "See you around."

Nate wandered over to his parents and Aunt Lizzie. "Great goal!" his parents enthused. Nate had almost forgotten his goal.

His aunt seemed to read Nate's mind. "Hey, what's with the Monarchs?" she asked. "Why didn't they give you the ball back after you kicked it out of bounds?"

Nate shrugged his shoulders. Suddenly he felt very tired. "I guess they didn't know they were supposed to."

"That's a bogus way to play." Aunt Liz put her arm around Nate's shoulder. "Don't worry. I'm proud of you. You played it the right way. That's what's important."

Nate glanced back at the scoreboard one more time. There was nothing he could do to change the score: 1–1. A tie.

Standing on the sidelines with the cool wind sweeping across the fields, Nate went over the game again in his mind. His goal. Hunter's equalizer. Luke's injury. Nate could almost see the open path to the goal before him again. Then he remembered making the decision to kick the ball out of bounds.

He still wondered: had he played it the right way?

W e'd better clear the table," Nate's father said as he pushed back his chair.

Nate grabbed the plates and slipped them into the dishwasher. "When do you think Mom will get home from her office?" he asked.

"She'll be out pretty late. She has to prepare for that conference in Atlanta next week."

Nate placed the silverware in the plastic rack.

"By the way, how was practice today?" his father asked.

Nate grabbed a sponge and wiped the kitchen counter. "Okay, I guess," he said.

"Sergio was still making noises about me kicking the ball out of bounds against the Monarchs."

His father waved it off. "Don't let him give you a hard time. Lizzie said you played it right. *She* should know." He pointed to the steps leading upstairs. "Go on and do your homework. I'll finish up in here."

Nate sat down at his computer to start his assignment, but he decided to check his e-mail first. "Hey," he said to himself softly, "I wonder what this is from Lizzie." He opened the message.

From:	Elizabeth Cooney
Subject:	Soccer film
Date:	October 26
To:	Nate Osborne

Hey, Nate—
I was talking to another sportswriter today about your game and the whole out-of-bounds thing. He sent me this YouTube link to a pro soccer game recorded a couple of years ago.

Thought you might like it. Maybe you can show it to Sergio to get him off your case. See you this weekend.

Aunt Lizzie
BTW...I told my teammates I'm a goal behind in our bet. So watch out, they're going to feed me the ball...BIG TIME!

Nate chuckled. *Lizzie sure wants to win that bet.*

He clicked on the link. The film of a soccer game appeared on the screen. One team was in yellow jerseys and the other in red. An announcer speaking in a foreign language shouted over the noise from the stadium crowd. A player in yellow was lying on the pitch, holding his ankle. A forward on the red team kicked the ball from fifty yards out toward the yellow team's goalkeeper.

He's giving them the ball back, Nate thought. *Just like Lizzie said you should.*

But the ball flew over the keeper's head

and into the yellow team's goal. "I don't believe it!" Nate blurted out. "The red team scored!"

The slow-motion instant replay showed the goal again. The ball sailed perfectly into the upper corner of the net. The red-shirted forward held his hands to his sides as if to say he had not meant to score the goal. Harsh whistles from the stadium crowd filled the air. The crowd was not happy.

The game started again. A yellow team defender skipped a long pass down the pitch. A yellow forward raced ahead and controlled the ball with a quick touch just before it bounced over the end line. He spun and after a touch or two kicked the ball into the wide-open red team's net. The red team's defense and goalkeeper did not make a move to stop him.

Nate watched the tape again. His brain could barely make sense of what he was seeing.

"Man, the red team let the yellow team score a goal just to make things fair," Nate said out loud. "I guess that's what Lizzie meant by winning the right way."

He pulled his chair closer to his computer. He clicked on the forward button and typed out an e-mail to Sergio.

From: Nate Osborne
Subject: Soccer film
Date: October 26
To: Sergio Hernandez

My aunt sent me this really cool soccer clip (see link below). You should definitely watch it...just so you know I'm not completely nuts about the out-of-bounds thing.

See you at school. We'd better beat the Rush on Saturday.

Later,
Nate

Get back!" the Strikers coach shouted. "Get back!"

Nate raced downfield, trying to catch up with the action. He shot a quick glance at the scoreboard.

STRIKERS   RUSH

2   4:20 HALF 1
            2

The Strikers were ahead 2–1 with only a few minutes to play, but the Rush were on the attack. Nate and his teammates were working hard to hang on to the lead.

Nate stretched his leg out for a steal and missed. The Rush midfielder floated a threatening ball toward the Strikers goal. Nate held his breath as Cam snapped the ball out of the air and tossed a quick pass to Sergio near the middle of the pitch.

Nate stopped, turned, and raced upfield. Sergio drove a long pass down the middle, hoping to catch the Rush by surprise.

His strategy worked! The ball floated past the Rush defenders. Nate gathered it in at full stride and barreled toward the Rush goal. Looking up from the ball, Nate could see the Rush keeper coming out of the goal to challenge the breakaway.

Nate touched the ball forward...a little too far. The keeper took two quick steps and leaped headlong for the ball. He grabbed it just as Nate was about to regain control. The keeper rolled on his side with the ball safely tucked to his chest. Nate tumbled over the keeper and rolled several times in the hard dirt and worn grass near the Rush net.

Nate looked at the referee, wondering if he might call a dangerous play penalty. But the ref called, "Play on!" The ball was already headed in the other direction.

Nate hustled back, slapping the dirt off his white shorts as he ran. The Rush were on the attack again, buzzing around the Strikers goal. The ball skipped across the end line.

The referee blew his whistle. "Corner kick!" he called, pointing to the corner.

"Get back! Get back!" Coach Lyn shouted, frantically waving his arms. Nate sprinted downfield to help on defense. He glanced at the clock. *Less than two minutes to go,* he thought. *If we can clear it out of our zone we may hang on to win...and get three points.*

The scene in front of the Strikers goal was chaos. Players pushed to get position while other players shouted instructions.

"Mark somebody!"

"Pick 'em up!"

"Look out for number 10!"

The ball soared into the clutch of players. A header sent the ball down toward the players' feet. It pinballed around until the ball squirted past Nate to the top of the penalty area. A Rush defender stepped up and blasted a low shot toward the goal. Somehow the ball squeezed its way through the tangle of arms and legs.

Cameron leaped to his left. Too late. The ball tucked inside the post and settled in the corner of the net.

Goal!

Nate and Sergio looked up helplessly, their faces twisted in agony as the Rush celebrated around them. "You've got to be kidding me!" Sergio shouted to the sky.

The score was tied, 2–2.

Cam fished the ball out of the net.

"Come on, come on!" Coach Lyn shouted. "Hurry up. We still have time."

But the ball was hardly back in play when the referee blew his whistle and crossed his arms above his head. The game was over at 2–2. Another tie.

Coach Lyn tried to keep up the team's spirits. "We've still got one more game," he pointed out. "You guys played well. The bounces just didn't go our way. We've still got a chance. We just have to practice and play even harder next week."

Nate, Sergio, and Cameron walked away from the pitch in a daze. The tie felt as heavy as a loss.

"I can't believe that last shot made it through all those players," Cam said, shaking his head. "I never saw it until the last second. And then it was too late."

"It's not your fault," Nate said, remembering how the ball had skipped by him. "We never should have let him get the shot."

"Man, another tie," Sergio said. "They should have overtime or shoot-outs or something. Anything but another tie."

Nate looked around the SoccerPlex. The fields were filled with teams of all ages. "They've got to get all the games in," he said. "No way they could play a bunch of overtimes. Anyway, I think shoot-outs are kind of bogus. I mean, letting someone run up on a wide-open shot from twelve yards away isn't really soccer."

"You can say that again," Cam said.

"So where are we in the standings?" Sergio asked.

Nate took out his phone and pulled up the website. The league standings appeared on the screen.

Team	Wins	Losses	Ties	Points
Monarchs	7	0	1	22
Devils	6	1	1	19
Strikers	5	0	3	18

Sergio looked away from the screen. "Man, we're in *third place!*"

"Yeah, but the Devils play the Monarchs next week," Nate noted. "The Monarchs will beat 'em, and when they do we'll be back in second place—and in the championship game—if we can get a win against the Barracudas."

"Why should the Monarchs beat the Devils?" Sergio asked. "Win, lose, or tie, the Monarchs are already in the championship game. They're not going to beat the Devils just for us."

"What are the times for the games next week?" Cameron asked.

Nate tapped some keys and the league schedule for the next Saturday appeared.

Saturday—November 12

9:00 a.m.	United v. Vipers
10:30 a.m	Monarchs v. Devils
Noon	Strikers v. Barracudas
1:30 p.m.	Rapids v. Sharks
3:00 p.m.	Sabres v. Rush

"The Monarchs play at 10:30 a.m. and we play at noon," Nate said.

Sergio let out a disappointed sigh. "At least we'll know before the game if we have a chance to play for the championship."

"We'll have a chance," Nate said, trying to sound certain.

"How can you be so sure?" Cam asked.

"Because we're going to be here at 10:30 and root like crazy for the Monarchs," Nate said.

Sergio groaned. "Man, things are worse than I thought."

"What do you mean?"

"I mean now we actually have to root *for* the Monarchs!"

Chapter 14

Let's go, Monarchs! Come on, hustle back! Get the ball!"

"Comeback time!"

Nate checked the scoreboard for the millionth time.

Nothing had changed. The Monarchs still

MONARCHS   **DEVILS**

1   5:05 HALF 2

trailed 2–1 with just five minutes to play. Nate could feel time—and the Strikers' hopes of playing in the championship game—slipping away.

The Monarchs had scored first, grabbing the lead on a sweet goal by Hunter Thomas, who'd redirected a low, skidding pass into the back of the net. But then the Monarchs seemed to relax and the Devils came charging back with two unanswered goals. They had kept the action in the Monarchs end of the pitch for most of the game.

Standing on the sidelines with Sergio and Cameron, Nate felt helpless. There was nothing he could do but scream for the Monarchs at the top of his lungs. And his cheers couldn't change the cold truth. If the Monarchs didn't come back to tie or win, it didn't matter what the Strikers did in their noon game against the Barracudas.

They would be out of the championship game.

"Come on! Get the ball!"

"Need a goal."

"Keep working, Monarchs!"

Sergio kicked the dirt. "I told you they're not going to win," he said, almost spitting the words out. "The Monarchs don't care. They know they're already in the championship game. Hunter and those guys aren't going to beat the Devils just for us. I'm betting they don't even want to play us again."

"There's still time," Cam said.

"Dig deep, Monarchs!" Nate yelled.

"Go for the goal, Hunter!"

"Put some pressure on."

Luke Jaworski stepped in front of a Devils crossing pass and bolted upfield. He dribbled past a couple of defenders and slipped a pass to Hunter on the left. The Monarchs forward controlled the ball with the slightest touch, then cut sharply to the right to create space between him and the defender. Hunter brought his right leg back and drove a hard shot toward the upper right-hand corner of the net.

Nate stood with his mouth wide open and his eyes as big as dinner plates. The Devils goalkeeper leaped straight out, his hands stretching for the ball. The ends of his fingers glanced against the ball.

But the ball had too much pace for him.

It changed course only slightly and sailed into the upper corner of the net.

Goal! The game was tied, 2–2.

Nate, Sergio, and Cameron jumped up and down, celebrating as if their favorite team had won the World Cup.

They had barely stopped cheering when Hunter aimed a crossing pass to the front of the Devils goal. Taj Oquendo, a Monarchs forward, leaped and snapped his head forward, sending the ball into the back of the net.

Another goal! The Monarchs had scored again.

"Yes!" Nate shouted and thrust a fist into the air.

"I don't believe it," Sergio said.

Nate was almost laughing. "Yeah, I thought you said the Monarchs wouldn't beat the Devils for us."

"Okay, okay." Sergio held up his hands in surrender. "I'm so happy to be wrong."

"Come on," Cam said. "They've got this game won. Let's go over to our field and get warmed up. We've still got to win our game."

Nate could barely feel his feet touching the ground as the three friends ran over to the field. They saw some Strikers warming up and gave them the news.

"The Monarchs won!"

"What was the score?"

"They came from behind to score two goals in the last minute and won 3–2. We're in the championship game if we win today."

The news of the Monarchs win surged through the team like a bolt of electricity, giving them a burst of energy. The Strikers warmed up at a faster pace, and it seemed like they couldn't wait to get on the pitch.

Sure enough, their team went on the attack right away, passing the ball and always staying a step ahead of the Barracudas. The Strikers kept the ball moving—to the wing...back to the defense...into the middle...back to the wing, where Nate lifted a centering pass that found Anton in front for a header.

Thunk! The net jumped back.

Goal! The Strikers were ahead 1–0 after two minutes.

Still, they didn't let up. Sergio stole a pass near midfield and burst by two defenders, then blasted a shot on goal. The ball dipped at the last moment and bounced off the diving goalkeeper's chest, spinning wildly near the face of the goal.

Sensing the opportunity, Nate swooped in from the wing and knocked it into the net with a swift left-footed touch.

Goal!

As Nate ran toward the sideline and skidded along his knees in celebration, he knew.

The Strikers were ahead 2–0.

There was no way his team was going to lose today.

The Strikers were going to play in the championship game.

Nate looked across the locker room and saw Hunter lacing up his sneakers.

"Hey, Hunter!" he called. "Thanks for saving the Strikers season on Saturday."

Hunter looked up. "We didn't do it for you guys," he explained. "We just didn't want to lose to the Devils."

Sergio slammed his locker shut. "We'll make you regret it," he said. "On Saturday."

"We'll see."

The class hustled out of the locker room into the gym, where Coach Roland was shouting in an excited voice. "Come on, let's go! We got a lot to do today. Move it. Move it!"

"Wonder why he's so crazed," Cameron said.

Nate pointed at the strips of tape stuck about ten yards apart on the gym floor. "I think I know," he said.

Coach Roland moved to the middle of the gym and clapped his hands. "Hustle up, guys," he said. "We're timing the shuttle run today. We're going to see how quick and agile you are. So let's get warmed up and do some stretching."

As Nate looked for a space on the crowded gym floor to warm up, he felt someone grab his elbow. It was Hunter.

"Last time we tied," he said. "How about the same bet today?"

"What do you mean?"

"Roland's going to time us in the shuttle run. So how about the four Monarchs against the four Strikers again?"

"To get warmed up for Saturday?" Nate smiled.

"Yeah, something like that."

Nate did some quick calculations. *We've got a good chance to beat those guys this time. Sergio and I are fast. Cam isn't that fast, but he's pretty quick. And so's Stevie.*

"So, same deal. If we win, you guys have to buy each of us an ice cream sandwich," Hunter said, interrupting Nate's thoughts and reviewing the terms of the bet.

"Okay, but if we—"

"Right," Hunter agreed. "We buy yours if you win." He put out his hand. "Bet?"

Nate shook Hunter's hand. "Bet," he said. Then he slipped over to where Sergio, Cameron, and Stevie were stretching and explained the bet in a low voice. The boys nodded. They were all in.

After they'd run a couple of quick laps around the gym, Coach Roland blew his whistle and shouted, "Line up against the wall and count off by fours!"

Nate made sure he would be teamed with the other Strikers. He could see Hunter and his teammates doing the same thing.

Coach Roland continued with his instructions. "Most of you have done this before. The tape on the floor is set ten yards apart. The idea is that you run across the gym four times." For emphasis he held up four fingers. "Be sure you touch the tape. If you don't, that's a three-second penalty. Two guys from each group will be judges. They'll stand right there to make sure you touch the tape. Everybody understand? Okay, let's go!"

The boys broke into their four-man teams. "I'll go first," Sergio said. "Get us off to a good start. And Nate, why don't you go last to nail down the win?"

Nate nodded and walked over to the tape on the far side of the gym to take his place as one of the judges.

"Judges, if the runner doesn't touch the tape, raise your hand," Coach Roland said in his final instructions. "Okay, runners get ready. On your mark...get set...go!"

Sergio bolted across the gym. He reached out and touched the tape and scrambled back a step ahead of the other runners. When Sergio came back, he reached out again. This time, Nate could see several inches of the wooden floor between Sergio's fingertips and the tape.

Sergio hadn't touched the tape!

Nate's hand shot up to signal a penalty.

Sergio blew across the finish line several steps ahead of the other runners. But his satisfied smile disappeared when he turned and saw Nate's hand in the air. He was steaming when he walked up to Nate.

"Why'd you call a penalty on me?"

"You missed the tape," Nate said, just stating the facts. "By a lot. I had to call it."

"Yeah, but that's a three-second penalty. We'll never win now."

"We'll make it up," Nate said as the runners and judges switched places and got ready for the next round. "And who knows, maybe the Monarchs will get a penalty."

"Yeah right." Nate could hear anger in Sergio's voice. "Like when they gave us the ball back after you kicked it out of bounds? No way the Monarchs are calling a penalty on themselves."

"They beat the Devils for us instead of throwing the game to help themselves later, didn't they?" Nate said. Sergio didn't say a thing.

Cameron and Stevie ran their races. Their times were good, not great, and they touched the tape each time. The Monarchs didn't have any penalties in their second and third races. Nate knew he had some time to make up as he toed the starting line.

"You'd better turn on the jets," Sergio said, eyeing the stopwatch in his hand. "We're probably way behind the Monarchs because of that stupid penalty."

Nate didn't say anything. He looked across the gym and saw Hunter getting ready to make his run, two lanes away. Nate was determined to run the best time he could. *Maybe I can at least beat Hunter,* he thought.

"On your mark…get set…go!"

Nate burst off the line. He stopped just short of the tape, reached out, and felt the tape under his fingertips. Then he dashed back in the other direction. Three more times across the gym, and Nate flashed across the finish line a good two steps ahead of Hunter.

Nate bent over to catch his breath. When he looked up he got a shock. Two lanes over, Luke Jaworski was standing with his hand in the air.

The Monarchs were calling a penalty on themselves!

"Good work, guys!" Coach Roland called. "I'll post the times on the wall outside the gym. Now get ready for your next class."

As the boys filed out of the gym and into the locker room, Nate stopped Luke. "What happened on the last race?" he asked.

The Monarch player shrugged and looked over at Hunter.

"I guess I messed up and missed the tape," Hunter said.

"And I had to call it," Luke added.

Nate didn't say anything. But the look on his face must have told the Monarchs what he was thinking.

"Don't be so surprised," Luke said. "You did the same thing."

"Yeah," Hunter agreed. "And you kicked the ball out of bounds when Luke got hurt, remember?" He pushed open the door to the locker room. "Listen," he called back, "we want to beat you, not cheat you."

After class, Nate found Sergio standing in front of the times posted on the wall. He showed Nate the total times on the calculator on his phone.

Nate	8.7	Hunter	11.8*
Sergio	11.9*	Luke	9.1
Stevie	9.1	Taj	9.3
Cam	9.4	Mikael	9.5
Total	39.1		39.7

* Three-second penalty added

"We won!" Sergio said. "By less than a second."

"That means the Monarchs would have won if they hadn't..." Nate didn't finish his sentence.

"Yeah," Sergio said. Then he saw what Nate was looking at. Hunter and Luke were emerging from the locker room. "Looks like you guys are buying," he said, letting them look at the times on his phone.

Hunter checked the numbers. "I guess so," he said. "But don't expect us to be that easy on you on Saturday."

Chapter 16

Nate sat on the grassy sideline catching his breath. He gulped another cup of cold water, crumpled the cup, and tossed it in a nearby basket. He thought back on the first half of the championship game.

The Strikers had jumped out to an early lead when Nate had slipped a perfect pass to Anton, who was unguarded by the far post. Anton had blasted it into the back of the net.

The Monarchs had come right back to knot the score at 1–1 when Hunter leaped high and headed the ball into the goal off a corner kick.

Nate took a few deep breaths, trying to

regain his strength. The first half had been the toughest of the season by far. Even tougher than the first Monarchs game. Every ball was contested. Every player was giving 100 percent all of the time.

It was the kind of game Aunt Lizzie was always talking about. Both teams were playing at full strength and playing their best. It was the kind of game Lizzie said you would always remember.

"Heck of a game," Sergio said, almost reading Nate's mind. "But I sure hope we don't tie them again."

Nate laughed. "We can't," he said. "Remember? This is for the championship. We can't have a tie. If it's tied after regulation, we have a five-minute overtime. If it's still tied after that we go to a shoot-out."

"I don't want to go to a shoot-out," Sergio said. "I'd be so nervous I'd be peeing down my leg."

Nate laughed. "How 'bout Cam? The keeper is super nervous in a shoot-out." Nate struggled to his feet. He was already so tired that he wasn't sure he would last through an overtime. "I guess we'd better beat them now," he said.

Coach Lyn was already rallying the team. "Okay, same starters as the first half," he said, clapping his hands. "Let's go get 'em!"

As Nate walked back onto the pitch he could hear Lizzie's voice above all the other cheers.

"Come on, Nate! Thirty minutes. You can do it, Strikers! Just thirty minutes. Give it everything you've got."

The Monarchs came on aggressively right from the start, keeping the ball in the Strikers end and threatening to score. Stevie cleared a crossing pass away from the Strikers net. But it didn't go far. Luke Jaworski controlled it in open space and hooked a long shot into the far corner of the Strikers net. Cam didn't have a chance.

Goal!

The Strikers were behind, 2–1.

The Monarchs kept the pressure on for most of the second half, peppering the goal with shots. Only a couple of great saves by

Cameron kept the margin at one goal. Time was running out.

Nate waited near midfield for the ball and a chance to score. *Less than five minutes to go and the score is 2–1,* he thought. *I'd take a tie now, that's for sure.*

With just moments to go in the game, a chance finally appeared for the Strikers offense to do something. Sergio won a loose ball and started upfield. He looked for Nate on the right but passed off to Anton to the left.

Sensing a chance, Nate slipped inside of Luke's defense and rushed toward the net, angling in from the right.

Anton skidded a perfectly timed pass toward the front of the net. Still a half step in front of Luke, Nate slid out his right foot and pushed the ball to the far corner past the flatfooted Monarchs keeper.

Goal! The score was tied, 2–2.

The Strikers were still celebrating when the referee blew her whistle indicating the game was over and going into overtime.

The Strikers gathered around Coach

Lyn. The boys were bouncing up and down and bumping into each other as if they couldn't keep their excitement bottled up.

"Overtime. We've got five minutes to make something happen!" Coach Lyn shouted. "Sergio, look upfield. If you get a chance, take it to the goal." Coach Lyn's eyes settled on Nate and held up one finger. "Take some chances. Remember, it's sudden death. One goal wins the game. One play. One play will make all the difference."

Standing in the circle of players, Nate could hear his Aunt Lizzie's voice from the stands.

"Come on, Nate. Make a play!

"Go, Strikers!

"Let's see some hustle!"

Nate's opportunity came in the opening minutes of overtime. The Strikers controlled play and went on the attack. Sergio bounced a pass to Nate as he angled toward the top of the penalty area. Instead of trying to control the ball, Nate figured he would take a chance. He timed the bouncing ball and volleyed a hard shot toward the net.

Boom! The shot felt strong flying off Nate's right foot. The quick shot caught the Monarchs keeper by surprise. The ball was headed toward the right corner when it swerved farther right and whistled by the post.

Nate had missed a goal by a few inches!

The Monarch keeper's long kick put his team back on the attack. A series of sharp passes had the Monarchs threatening near the top of the penalty box. Hunter Thomas gained control with his chest. Then with the ball at his feet and his back to the Strikers goal, he faked left, creating just a sliver of space. Hunter pushed the ball, spun right, and drilled a low shot.

Cameron leaped almost parallel to the ground and stretched out as far as he could. Too late! The ball whizzed by his gloved hands and into the net.

At the instant the ball pushed back the net, everything changed, like a huge wave sweeping away a carefully built sandcastle. Hunter and the Monarchs leaped into the air and into each other's arms. The crowd burst into cheers. Cam lay facedown on the ground, pounding his fists into the dirt. The Strikers stood shocked and not sure what to do or where to go.

Nate suddenly felt exhausted. His legs could hardly hold him up.

The game was over.

The Monarchs had won.

The Strikers' hopes of winning the U-14 championship were gone.

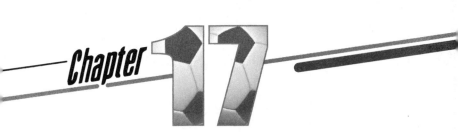

Chapter 17

Nate stared at the piece of paper. Some of the numbers and words looked like a foreign language to him.

"What's 'tsp' stand for?" he asked.

"Teaspoon."

Nate held up two spoons. "So which one is the teaspoon?"

"The smaller one. The other one's a tablespoon." Aunt Lizzie reached into the cupboard and pulled out a mixing bowl.

Nate looked at the recipe again.

OATMEAL CHOCOLATE CHIP COOKIES

Mix together the following ingredients:

½ cup butter

1½ cups rolled oats

¾ cup all-purpose flour

½ cup brown sugar

1 egg

1 tsp vanilla

½ tsp salt

¼ cup sugar

¼ tsp baking soda

Chocolate chips and walnuts

Preheat oven to 350 degrees. Mix ingredients in a large mixing bowl. Place spoonfuls of cookie dough two inches apart on a cookie sheet. Cook for 8–10 minutes or until lightly browned. Use a spatula to remove to a cooling rack until cool.

"How much is a half cup of butter?" Nate asked.

"One stick. See, it says it right here," Lizzie said, pointing to the paper wrapped around the butter. "I like to melt the butter first. It makes the mixing easier. We'll just add some extra flour so the mixture won't get too soupy."

They started mixing the ingredients together, carefully measuring out the amounts.

"This mixing's not that easy," Nate said as he pushed a large spoon around the side of the mixing bowl. "This is a pretty good workout."

"Wait," Lizzie said. "Let me get a couple of pictures. Remember? Your mom said she wanted to see you making cookies." Lizzie grabbed her phone and snapped a few quick shots. "I'll e-mail them to her. She'll get a kick out of you mixing the batter."

Lizzie took a long look at the contents of the mixing bowl. "Do you want to put in some walnuts?" she asked.

"Sure, I like nuts. How many chocolate chips should we put in?"

"I like to put in about a third to half a bag. But we won't need that many if we're going to add the walnuts too. Did you remember the baking soda?"

Nate nodded. "Don't worry, I remembered everything." His hands were dusted white with flour. He dropped a glob of cookie dough off a spoon and onto the cookie sheet, then licked the edge of the spoon.

"Hey, don't eat all the dough," Lizzie protested, handing him a clean spoon. "Remember, I won the bet. They're my cookies."

A few minutes after Nate and Lizzie placed the cookies in the oven, the kitchen began to fill with the sweet smells of chocolate, sugar, and butter. As they waited for the timer to buzz, Nate and Lizzie talked about their soccer seasons.

"I can't believe you scored three goals in your last game," Nate said. "You must've really wanted to win our bet."

Lizzie smiled. "Don't worry, I'll share the cookies with you."

"I'm not worried about me, but I promised Sergio some cookies if I won," Nate said. "He'll probably give me grief for losing the bet."

"We'll save him a few." Lizzie opened the oven door to check the cookies. "A couple more minutes," she said, closing the door. "Is Sergio still giving you a hard time about kicking the ball out of bounds?"

"Not really. I think that film link you sent helped," Nate said. "Anyway, I think he probably just wanted to play the Monarchs for the championship."

"That was a terrific game," Lizzie said. "You guys played great. I thought it was your best game of the season."

"Yeah, but I still wish we had won."

"You played your best against a good team. You can live with that." Lizzie checked the oven timer. "Why don't you check the cookies? They should be done by now." She handed him the oven mitts.

"Come on, you should be doing some of the work. After all, you *lost* the bet."

Nate pulled the cookie sheet out of the oven and took a deep breath over the cookies, taking in all their sweetness. He slipped a spatula under one and let it slide onto the rack.

When he had finished transferring the cookies, he started to reach for one.

"Wait, we've got to let them cool," Lizzie said.

"How long?"

"Not too long." Lizzie looked at Nate. "Is that kid Hunter going to play with you on the high school freshman team next year?"

"Yeah, we should have him and me up front, Sergio in the middle, Cameron in the goal, Stevie and Luke on defense—"

"Whoa, you guys should have a really good team," Lizzie said. "I don't think I'll make the same bet with you next year. With you and Hunter up front, you may score a million goals."

Lizzie touched the top of a warm cookie. "Ready," she declared, handing one to Nate.

As he savored the rich, chocolaty taste, Nate thought back on the Strikers season: The wins, the ties. The mile run competition. Lizzie explaining why you should kick the ball out of bounds. The soccer video. The surprise comeback by the Monarchs that got the Strikers into the championship game. The shuttle run race in gym class. The last painful overtime loss. The bet with Lizzie. All the ups and downs.

Nate had started the season wanting to beat the Monarchs more than anything. But now, remembering the great game the Strikers and Monarchs had played, with everyone on both teams giving it everything they had, losing didn't seem quite as bad as he'd thought it would be.

Nate reached for another cookie. "Things turned out all right," he said.

"You mean the cookies?" Lizzie asked.

"Yeah, the cookies." Nate smiled. "And everything else."

The Real Story

Although it seems hard to believe, the game described on pages 82 and 83 really happened. The match was between AFC Ajax and SC Cambuur during the 2006 season in the top Dutch professional league *(Eredivisie)*.

An Ajax player, Jan Vertonghen, was returning the ball to Cambuur after the play had stopped for an injury. Vertonghen was too strong with the pass to his opponent and the ball sailed over the shocked Cambuur keeper and ended up in the net. Even though the players had stopped playing, the goal counted.

After the kickoff, to make things even, Ajax allowed Cambuur to score. They stood to the side as a Cambuur forward knocked the ball into the net. The Ajax players didn't want to win because of an injury and an accidental goal.

There are other instances of exceptional sportsmanship on the soccer pitch. In a 2000 English Premier League match, a West Ham United FC striker, Paolo Di Canio, passed up the opportunity to score the winning goal by catching the ball instead of knocking it into the net because the Everton FC goalkeeper, Paul Gerrard, was lying injured in front of the goal. FIFA, the world federation of soccer, later commended Di Canio for this remarkable display of fair play.

Another part of the story reflected a situation that happened in real life. Just as the Monarchs came back to win a game to save their rival team's playoff hopes, the United States men's World Cup team rallied to win a game to keep the World Cup hopes of Mexico, its archrival, alive.

During the 2014 World Cup qualifying

rounds, the U.S. had already secured a spot as one of the teams from the CONCACAF (North and Central Americas) region going to the 32-team World Cup in Brazil. The U.S. team would play one more game with Panama at the Estadio Rommel Fernandez in Panama City.

If Panama could beat the United States, they would qualify for fourth place in the CONCACAF region and play a playoff game with New Zealand for a chance to move on to the World Cup. But if Panama lost to the U.S., Mexico would be the fourth-place team and would still have a chance to go to the World Cup. Panama had everything to play for, while the U.S. men did not seem to have any reason to play their hardest. After all, they had already qualified for the World Cup.

With only a short time left in the game, Panama led 2–1. The Panamanian fans at the stadium were on their feet and ready to celebrate.

But the United States team did not stop playing their best. The Americans scored twice in the final few minutes on goals by Graham Zusi and Aron Johannsson to pull out a 3–2 win and break Panama's heart.

Now it was Mexico's turn to celebrate because their World Cup chances were still alive. Mexican newspapers the next day ran headlines saying "THANK YOU!" "WE LOVE YOU," and "GOD BLESS AMERICA."

Eventually Mexico went to the World Cup and won two out of three games in Group A to move on to the knockout rounds. Mexico lost to the Netherlands 2–1 in its Round of 16 match. (The United States lost to Belgium 2–1 in the same round.)

Examples of good sportsmanship can be found across all sports. Another remarkable story of fair play occurred in a 2008 softball playoff game between Western Oregon University (WOU) and Central Washington University (CWU). Early in the game, WOU trailed 2–1 but had two runners on base. Right fielder Sarah Tucholsky came to the plate and belted the second pitch over the fence for a three-run homer.

The 5' 2" Tucholsky had never hit a home run in either high school or college. In her excitement, she missed first base. As she turned back to touch the bag, her knee gave way and she collapsed. Tucholsky crawled to first base but could not go any further because of the pain in her injured knee.

Tucholsky and WOU had a big problem. As the WOU first-base coach explained, the rules stated that teammates and coaches are not allowed to touch base runners. The injured player would be called out if her WOU teammates tried to help her. The umpire said the WOU coach could substitute a pinch runner for Tucholsky, but in that case her over-the-fence home run would only count as a single.

Then something surprising and wonderful happened. The CWU first baseman, Mallory Holtman, asked the umpire if she and her teammates could help Tucholsky around the bases. The umpire said there was no rule against it.

So Holtman and CWU shortstop Liz Wallace carefully placed their arms under

Tucholsky's legs. The WOU right fielder put her arms over her opponents' shoulders. The three young women headed around the base paths. The CWU players stopped and gently lowered Tucholsky to let her touch each base—second, third, and home—with her uninjured leg.

Tucholsky had her home run and WOU went on to win the game 4–2. The CWU team lost its chance to win the conference and to advance in the playoffs. But the CWU players did not want to win because someone got injured on a play. "It was the right thing to do," CWU's Holtman said later. "She'd hit it over the fence. She deserved the home run."

The young women on the CWU softball team understood what Aunt Lizzie tried to teach Nate and the other Strikers: A real athlete does not want to win because they took advantage of an opponent's injury. Real athletes want to earn the win fairly when their opponents are at their best and playing their hardest.

A real athlete wants to win the *right* way.

SPECIAL THANKS

*The author would like to thank the following
people for their help with this book:*

*Steven Goff, soccer reporter extraordinaire
for the* Washington Post, *shared his encyclopedic
knowledge of the beautiful game over lunch one day
at McGinty's in Silver Spring, Maryland.*

*Len Oliver, member of the National Soccer
Hall of Fame and longtime leader of the D. C.
Stoddert youth soccer league, told me stories about
soccer (and other sports) in the 1950s over coffee
one sunny afternoon. I can only hope he enjoyed
the afternoon as much as I did.*

*The information about the examples of good
sportsmanship contained in "The Real Story" came
from articles in the* Independent, *the* London Evening
Standard, *the* Huffington Post, *and* CBSNews.com.

About the Author

FRED BOWEN was a Little Leaguer who loved to read. Now he is the author of many action-packed books of sports fiction. He has also written a weekly sports column for kids in the *Washington Post* since 2000.

Fred played lots of sports growing up, including soccer at Marblehead High School. For thirteen years, he coached kids' baseball, soccer, and basketball teams. Some of his stories spring directly from his coaching experience and his sports-happy childhood in Marblehead, Massachusetts.

Fred holds a degree in history from the University of Pennsylvania and a law degree from George Washington University. He was a lawyer for many years before retiring to become a full-time children's author. Bowen has been a guest author at schools and conferences across the country, as well as the Smithsonian Institute in Washington, DC, and The Baseball Hall of Fame.

Fred lives in Silver Spring, Maryland, with his wife Peggy Jackson. Their son is a college baseball coach and their daughter is a graduate student in Colorado studying to become a teacher.

For more information
check out the author's website at
www.fredbowen.com.

HEY, SPORTS FANS!

Don't miss these action-packed books by Fred Bowen...

Want more?

All-Star Sports Story Series

T. J.'s Secret Pitch
PB: $5.95 / 978-1-56145-504-1

T. J.'s pitches just don't pack the power they need to strike out the batters, but the story of 1940s baseball hero Rip Sewell and his legendary eephus pitch may help him find a solution.

The Golden Glove
PB: $5.95 / 978-1-56145-505-8

Without his lucky glove, Jamie doesn't believe in his ability to lead his baseball team to victory. How will he learn that faith in oneself is the most important equipment for any game?

The Kid Coach
PB: $5.95 / 978-1-56145-506-5

Scott and his teammates can't find an adult to coach their team, so they must find a leader among themselves.

Playoff Dreams
PB: $5.95 / 978-1-56145-507-2

Brendan is one of the best players in the league, but no matter how hard he tries, he can't make his team win.

Winners Take All
PB: $5.95 / 978-1-56145-512-6

Kyle makes a poor decision to cheat in a big game. Someone discovers the truth and threatens to reveal it. What can Kyle do now?